SECRETS FROM A BIG BROTHER

Walter couldn't believe it. His big-shot brother, Danny, never played with him anymore. Now Danny wanted to hit a few with Walter. Danny was a real slugger. Maybe he could help Walter be one, too.

Danny pitched three slow ones. Walter was late on the first two. He tagged the third.

"Stop trying for a grand slam and just get the bat on the ball," said Danny.

Walter tried again but he wasn't much better.

Danny walked across the lawn to him. "Wanna know how you can always hit the ball?"

Walter looked up at Danny and waited for the secret.

"One word," said Danny. "Bunt. You won't make a home run, but it's a good shot at getting on first. And you'll always make a hit."

You'll always make a hit. The words sounded like magic. This could be Walter's secret weapon. He couldn't wait to try it out.

Other Bantam Skylark Books you will enjoy
Ask your bookseller for the books you have
  missed

THE CHOCOLATE TOUCH
    by Patrick Skene Catling
ELIZABETH'S SUPER-SELLING
    LEMONADE (Sweet Valley Kids #9)
    by Francine Pascal
ENCYCLOPEDIA BROWN AND THE
    CASE OF THE DISGUSTING
    SNEAKERS by Donald J. Sobol
MOLLY'S PILGRIM by Barbara Cohen
THE WHITE STALLION
    by Elizabeth Shub
THUNDER AT GETTYSBURG
    by Patricia Gauch

THE NEVER SINK NINE

Slugger Mike

BY GIBBS DAVIS

Illustrated by
George Ulrich

A BANTAM SKYLARK BOOK©
NEW YORK • TORONTO • LONDON • SYDNEY • AUCKLAND

RL 2, 005-008

SLUGGER MIKE
A Bantam Skylark Book / May 1991

Skylark Books is a registered trademark of Bantam Books,
a division of Bantam Doubleday Dell Publishing Group, Inc.
Registered in U.S. Patent and Trademark Office and elsewhere.

ISBN 0-553-15883-X

Published simultaneously in the United States and Canada

Bantam Books are published by Bantam Books, a division of Bantam Doubleday Dell
Publishing Group, Inc. Its trademark, consisting of the words "Bantam Books" and the
portrayal of a rooster, is Registered in U.S. Patent and Trademark Office and in other
countries. Marca Registrada. Bantam Books, 1540 Broadway, New York, New York 10036.

PRINTED IN THE UNITED STATES OF AMERICA

CWO   0 9 8 7 6 5 4

*For Robert, whose winning mitt sits
on my desk while I write stories
about the Never Sink Nine*

CHAPTER ONE

The Never Sink Eight

Walter Dodd's baseball bat fell off his bike.

"Rats!"

It was the fourth time this had happened since he left his house. Walter stopped to pick it up. He balanced the bat across his handlebars and headed for Diamond Park.

He was glad Grandpa Walt had called the Never Sink Nine together for team practice. He wanted to work on his hitting before their game with the Polar Blasts. Besides, there was nothing to do on Sunday—except homework.

Walter tried not to think about his book report. It was due a week from Monday.

A bike turned the corner ahead of him. It was his best friend Mike Lasky. He'd recognize Mike's head anywhere. His hair stuck out in patches. He was always getting bubble gum stuck in it. Then his mother or their teacher, Mrs. Howard, had to cut it out.

"Hey, Mike!" yelled Walter. "Wait up!"

Mike looked over his shoulder. His face was hidden by a big bubble of pink gum. He jammed on his brakes.

Walter stopped next to Mike and poked the bubble.

Pop!

Mike's nose appeared. It was covered with a white blob.

"Yuck," Walter said. "What's that goop on your face?"

"Sunburn stuff," said Mike. "My mom made me wear it."

"Good idea," Walter said. He turned

2

his baseball cap around. Usually he wore it backwards, but today the sun was too hot. His T-shirt was all sweaty.

"I'm burning up," Mike panted.

Walter reached into his backpack and pulled out his neon-orange, double-barreled water pistol. "Hey, Mike," he called.

Mike turned. Walter took aim and squirted him in the face.

Mike licked up the cool water. "Thanks. I needed that."

Walter gave his own face a squirt and stuck the water pistol back in his backpack. "It's a heat wave," said Walter. His mother had said that at breakfast.

Walter and Mike started pedaling up the street together.

"My dad just put in an air conditioner," said Mike.

"Lucky." Walter had a fan in his bedroom. His big brother Danny was always hogging it.

Mike shot ahead of Walter. "Race you to the park!" he yelled over his shoulder.

"No fair!" Walter held onto his bat with

3

one hand and chased Mike all the way to Diamond Park.

The boys left their bikes next to Grandpa Walt's old station wagon. Walter smiled. He knew his grandfather was the best coach their team could have. A long time ago he had played in the minors.

Walter spotted his grandfather carrying a heavy bag of baseball equipment across Willie Mays field. *It's a good thing he has strong arms,* thought Walter. Grandpa Walt kept himself in tip-top shape by swimming fifty laps at the YMCA every day.

Walter and Mike hurried over to help him.

Grandpa Walt wiped his forehead. "Worst heat wave since I was a boy," he groaned. "We'll make it a short one today."

"Here come the horse girls," said Walter.

Melissa Nichols and her younger sister Jenny pranced across the field like twin horses. As usual one of Melissa's toy horses poked out of her backpack.

Walter and Mike rolled their eyes at each other.

4

They found the rest of the Never Sink Nine waiting in the dugout. It was the only shady spot in Diamond Park.

Grandpa Walt turned to a boy whose leg was in a cast. "Ready for roll call, Tony?"

Tony Pappas couldn't play with a broken leg so Grandpa Walt gave him special jobs instead. In addition to taking roll call, Tony drew pictures of all the players on the team. He read off the first name on the list. "Billy Baskin."

No one answered.

Walter looked down at his baseball bat. He wished he could hit like Billy Baskin. Billy was the team slugger.

"He was late every practice last week," said Melissa, tossing her head like a pony. Melissa was their best pitcher.

Walter checked his official Babe Ruth wristwatch. "He's only twelve minutes and thirty-four seconds late."

Grandpa Walt smiled. "Thank you, Walter."

Walter smiled back. Ever since he got his watch he was always on time.

5

"I saw a goat in Billy's front yard on the way here," said Otis Hooper. "He was tied to a tree."

"Sure," said Mike. "A *billy* goat." He elbowed Walter and they laughed.

Otis shrugged. "See if I care if you don't believe me!" He opened his catcher's mask and shoved a chocolate bar in his mouth. Otis was always eating chocolate.

Tony finished taking roll call. Everyone was there except Billy.

"Let's get down to team business," said Grandpa Walt. "The Polar Blasts won their first game, too, so we've got our work cut out for us."

"Look!" Tony stood up on his crutches. "Here comes the Polar Blasts' team mascot!"

A large white dog was running across the field with a leash trailing behind him. Two of the Polar Blasts chased after him and grabbed the leash. They headed for the dugout and paraded their mascot past the Never Sink Nine.

"Show-offs," whispered Mike.

Walter nodded. But he wished they had a mascot, too.

"Here comes Beanpole Becky," said Otis.

A tall girl in a Polar Blasts cap stopped in front of the Never Sink Nine dugout.

"What's your mascot's name?" asked Melissa, waving a toy horse at the dog.

"Bear," said Becky, coolly. "Like polar bear. Get it?"

"Awesome," said Otis.

"Where's *your* team mascot?" Becky asked.

"We don't have one," said Jenny.

"We don't *need* one," said Mike.

"Every good team has one," Becky said, and turned away.

Melissa stood up. "Our team needs a mascot, too."

"Good idea," said Grandpa Walt. "Any suggestions?"

"I think we should have a horse," said Melissa. She reached into her backpack and pulled out a gray spotted horse. "I vote for Misty."

Walter and Mike groaned.

"Toy mascots are for babies," said Mike. "We need a *real* one. Like a tiger."

"Or a snake," said Walter.

"No snakes!" said Jenny, raising her feet. She checked under the bench.

"We'll vote on a team mascot later," said Grandpa Walt. "Time to warm up on the field."

"I'm already warmed up," said Otis, wiping his forehead. "My chocolate melted all over my mitt."

"Okay," said Grandpa Walt. "Let's get started. Melissa, Otis, Felix, and Katie take field positions. Everyone else line up for batting practice."

Jenny Nichols stepped up to home plate. She was the youngest player on the team. Melissa pitched a slow ball to her sister. Jenny closed her eyes and took a wild swing.

"Keep your eye on the ball," said Grandpa Walt. "Choke up on the bat." He took the bat and showed her.

9

Walter groaned. "She's gonna take forever."

"Look who's talking." Christy Chung peered at Walter through her big sunglasses that had little ballerinas on the sides.

Walter dug the toe of his sneaker into the dirt. He felt bad. He was a lousy hitter and everyone knew it. He watched Jenny take a wide swing at the ball and miss it. *At least I'm better than she is,* he thought.

"Thanks, Jenny," Grandpa Walt said. "We'll do some more later."

Jenny dragged her bat back to the dugout.

"Good try, Jen." Christy patted her shoulder.

"Next," said Grandpa Walt.

Walter grabbed his bat and ran to the batter's box. He lifted the bat and waited for the pitch.

"Whoa!" said Grandpa Walt. "Safety first." He handed Walter a batting helmet.

Walter shoved it on and took a practice swing.

Swooooosh! The bat made a small breeze.

"Ready?" called Melissa from the pitcher's mound.

Walter nodded. He grabbed the bat tightly. He'd show Christy. He'd show *everybody.*

Swooooosh! He swung too late and missed.

Then he swung again. And again.

"Is that Danny's old bat?" asked Grandpa Walt.

Walter nodded. His brother was the best hitter on his team. Walter had thought some of Danny's hitting power might rub off on him.

"Hang on." Grandpa Walt fished around in the equipment bag. He pulled out a shorter bat. "Try this for size."

Walter lifted the bat over one shoulder. It felt lighter.

"Come on, Walter!" shouted Mike from the dugout. "You can do it!"

Walter looked over his shoulder. Mike gave him a thumbs-up sign. *At least I can count on my best friend,* he thought.

Melissa wound up and pitched.

11

This time Walter's bat swung around fast. He felt a solid hit. A grounder bounced down the third-base line.

"Good going," said Grandpa Walt. "Looks like we've solved your problem."

After Walter finished his turn at bat Grandpa Walt took him off to one side. "What do you say we buy you a new bat this week?"

"Great!" said Walter. He loved doing things with his grandfather. And with a new bat he might get more hits than misses. He hurried back to the dugout and pulled a small notepad out of his backpack. SLUGGER SECRETS was penciled on the outside. He flipped to the first page and filled in number three.

He put five stars next to it for luck. Five was Walter's lucky number.

"What's that?" asked Christy. She was leaning over to see better.

"None of your beeswax." Walter slipped the notepad into the bottom of his backpack.

Christy held up a book with a picture of a ballerina on the cover. "I'm doing my book report on ballet. What's your book?"

Walter forgot his hitting success. "I haven't decided yet," he said sadly.

"You're going to be in big trouble," said Christy. "You didn't do the last book report."

"So what?" said Walter, covering a sneaker with dirt.

"So . . ." Christy flipped her long black hair over one shoulder. "Mrs. Howard could flunk you, like Otis."

Walter looked at Otis squatting behind home plate. He was supposed to be in fourth grade with Danny but Mrs. Howard had held him back a year.

13

Mike was next up to bat. He hit the first ball deep into the outfield.

"Way to go!" shouted Walter.

When Mike was finished he passed the batting helmet to Christy.

"You're almost as good as Billy," Christy said to Mike.

"Thanks." Mike blushed the bright pink of his bubble gum. He liked Christy. "I've been practicing." His face disappeared behind a large bubble of gum.

Walter wished somebody thought *he* was as good as Billy Baskin. But he didn't say anything.

After Christy took her turn at bat Grandpa Walt blew his whistle. "Change positions!" he shouted.

Walter and Mike grabbed their mitts and ran out onto the field. Walter went straight to second base.

"Walter!" shouted Grandpa Walt. "Take the mound! I want you to try pitching today."

Walter couldn't believe his ears. He

jogged to the pitcher's mound. *Grandpa Walt must really think I'm good,* he thought.

It was hard getting a tiny baseball over home plate. But after a few tries Walter began to get them in the strike zone.

Melissa gave Walter an A-OK sign. He felt great. Melissa was the best pitcher on the team.

After everyone had a turn at bat Grandpa Walt walked onto the field and everyone ran to gather around him. "That's it for today, team," he said. "Good work! Keep practicing hitting and throwing at home. And let's all look for a team mascot!"

Walter grabbed his backpack and ran to his bike. He and Mike usually raced each other to their bikes. But today Grandpa Walt kept Mike back to talk.

While Walter waited for his friend he thought about which kind of bat he wanted. Wood or aluminum? Maybe a Louisville Slugger or an Easton. He wondered if there were other, even better bats.

Mike jogged over to his bike. He

looked happy. "Coach says my hitting is getting real good. He says I should start practicing at the batting cage. Wanna go sometime?"

"Sure," said Walter. His grandfather was always trying to help kids on the team improve—especially the good players.

"Let's head over to Billy Baskin's and see what's going on," said Mike.

"Sounds good." Walter pushed off on his bike. He looked back at Mike pushing his mitt into his backpack. "Race you!" he shouted.

"No fair!" Mike slung his backpack over one shoulder and shoved off. He started pedaling double-time to catch up. "Hey, you had a head start!"

Walter knew Mike was right. But he didn't slow down. Walter loved to win. He didn't want Mike to be better at anything than he was, even if they *had* been best friends since kindergarten.

They cut across the Eleanor Roosevelt Elementary School parking lot and headed for Billy Baskin's house.

16

Walter turned onto Billy's street and saw a big moving van.

"Hey, what's going on?" shouted Mike.

The moving van was parked in front of Billy Baskin's house. In the front yard were piles of boxes and furniture.

A pink nose stuck up above a crate of books.

Walter moved closer. It was a four-legged animal with a beard. It was a goat!

The goat's mouth opened and a strange sound echoed up the street.

"Ba-a-a-a-a!"

Mike hopped off his bike and began to pet the goat's long, furry back. "Otis said there was a goat in Billy's yard, remember?"

Walter nodded. He touched the goat's stubby horns. "Otis sure was right," he said.

The goat tossed his head back and showed his teeth. "Ba-a-a-a-a-!"

Walter and Mike jumped back.

The goat moved forward and gently nudged Walter. It wagged its tail.

17

"Hi, guys!" Billy jumped down the front steps and ran to meet them. "I see you met Homer."

"Who?" said Walter.

"The goat," said Billy. "A guy named Pete tied him up here today. He's allergic to dogs, so he has a goat. It's the only pet that doesn't make him sneeze."

"Who's Pete?" asked Mike.

Billy stuffed his hands in his pockets and mumbled something. It sounded like, "He's moving into my house."

Walter and Mike stared at Billy, wide-eyed. "What?" they shouted at the same time.

"We're moving," said Billy with a sigh. "That's why I missed practice today."

"Why didn't you tell us?" Walter couldn't believe his ears.

"Yeah," said Mike. "What will the team do without you? You're our best hitter."

Billy shrugged. "I didn't tell anyone because I thought maybe my parents would change their minds."

Mrs. Baskin called from their front

door. "Five minutes, Billy. Then we leave." She waved to Walter and Mike. "We're going to miss you boys!"

Walter looked at the goat. Then he looked at the moving van. He couldn't decide which one was more of a surprise.

No one could think of anything to say. The only sound was the goat chewing grass.

"Guess I'd better go," said Billy, finally.

"Where're you moving?" Walter asked.

"Florida." Billy reached into his pocket and pulled out some scraps of paper. Each one had his new address written on it. He handed one to Mike and one to Walter. "Write me," he said. Then he jogged to his front door. He turned to wave good-bye. "Good luck with the team!" he called.

Walter and Mike petted the goat one last time and got on their bikes.

They bicycled toward home, side by side.

Mike was chewing gum a mile a minute. Walter knew that always meant his friend was thinking.

"What's our team gonna do without Billy?" said Mike. "We'll be the Never Sink *Eight*."

Walter knew a team had to have nine players to be in the Rockville League. They wouldn't even be allowed to play the Polar Blasts this Saturday. And what would they do without a team slugger?

"Billy's wrecked everything," said Mike. He split off from Walter to go home. "See you later, alligator."

"In a while, crocodile."

Walter pedaled slowly up Elm Street and thought about things. Their team slugger was gone. What good was a baseball team without a home-run hitter?

Walter looked down at Danny's old bat resting across his handlebars. He remembered what Grandpa Walt had said. All he needed was a new bat and he'd be slugging them over the fence. He pedaled a little faster.

"Me," he said, picking up speed. "*I'm* going to be the new team slugger!"

When he got home, Walter tossed Danny's old bat into the farthest-away corner of the garage. He wouldn't need it anymore.

CHAPTER TWO

Home-Run Homer

Monday morning meant one thing to Walter—Reading Hour.

Mrs. Howard walked up and down the aisles of their third grade classroom, picking students to read out loud.

Melissa Nichols had been reading forever. She was shouting to be heard above the *whir* of the fan. It was pointing directly at her.

Melissa hadn't made one mistake and she got to be cool, too. *Some people have all the luck,* thought Walter.

Walter blew down the neck of his sweaty T-shirt. He leaned across the aisle and whispered to Mike, "Watch this." He gave the backpack under Melissa's chair a little kick. The backpack was filled with toy horses.

Melissa looked up and stumbled over the word she was reading.

Mike gave Walter a thumbs-up sign. Both boys loved to tease Melissa.

Walter looked over at Billy Baskin's empty desk. He missed Billy already. He thought about getting his new bat with Grandpa Walt, and he felt a little better. Maybe he'd become as good a hitter as Billy.

"Look out," Mike whispered. Mrs. Howard was walking up their aisle.

Walter closed his eyes, crossed his fingers, and held his breath. He heard Mrs. Howard's skirt swish past his desk.

Safe. He opened one eye. Mrs. Howard stopped behind Mike. She lightly tapped his shoulder. That was the signal to start reading.

Mike began to read slowly and struggled with some of the words.

Walter let out a sigh of relief. He felt lucky today, and he wasn't even wearing the lucky socks Grandpa Walt had given him after their first practice game. He hadn't washed them for two weeks. Good luck was tricky. He didn't want to risk washing it out.

At the end of Reading Hour Mrs. Howard made an announcement. "Some of you already know a member of our class has moved away."

"Billy Baskin," said Mike before anyone else could.

"To Florida," added Walter.

Walter and Mike grinned at each other. They had been the first to know.

Mrs. Howard smiled at them. "What you *don't* know is a new classmate will be joining us today."

"Boy or girl?" asked Christy Chung.

"Boy, boy, boy, boy, boy," Walter whispered to himself. Lucky five might make it come true.

"His name is Peter Santos," said Mrs. Howard.

Walter reached across the aisle and gave Mike a high-five.

"Let's take this time before lunch to work on our book reports," said Mrs. Howard.

All the kids got out their books. Even Mike had one. Walter leaned over to read the title: *Encyclopedia Brown Takes the Case*. On the cover was a picture of a boy detective.

Christy Chung walked past Walter on her way to the pencil sharpener. She looked down at Walter's doodles of baseball bats and shook her head. "You'd better shape up or you know what will happen." Her eyes moved toward Otis Hooper.

Walter's heart sank. He remembered what Christy had said about flunking. Maybe he would flunk like Otis. Walter wondered if he could still be clean-up batter if he did badly in school.

A loud noise echoed through the room. It was coming from the open window.

"Ba-a-a-a-a! Ba-a-a-a-a!"

Walter and Mike looked at each other. "Homer!" they shouted together. They raced to the window with the rest of the class.

A tall boy in a baseball cap was tying a goat to a bush outside their classroom window. It was the same goat Walter and Mike had seen in Billy Baskin's front yard. Only today the goat wore a red bandana around his neck.

The boy looked up at Mrs. Howard's class. "Hi. I'm Pete Santos." He patted the goat's head. "This is Homer. He wanted to meet my new class."

Mrs. Howard was wide-eyed. Her mouth formed a big O but nothing came out.

Everyone was trying to reach through the open window to touch Homer.

"Can we go out and pet him?" asked Melissa.

"Please?" said Otis.

"*Pleeeeease?*" said everyone together.

Mrs. Howard looked doubtful. "I don't know, children. We're supposed to be inside until recess." She stuck her head out the

26

window. The flower pinned to her blouse fell to the ground. Homer quickly ate it and then moved over to a bed of daisies.

"Oh, my," said Mrs. Howard.

The whole class stared at Mrs. Howard. Finally, she smiled a big smile. "Oh, all right," she said. "It's not every day that a goat comes to visit. You can have a brief recess until lunchtime."

Everyone stampeded out the door.

Walter pushed through the crowd. "I saw your goat already," he said to Pete. "In Billy Baskin's yard."

"Me, too," said Mike, squeezing between them.

Walter looked at all the pins on Pete's baseball cap. Each one was from a different major league team. "Cool hat," he said.

"Thanks," said Pete. "Wanna hear a good joke?" he asked. "Why do baseball players stay so cool?"

Walter shrugged.

"Because they have a lot of fans."

Everyone laughed.

"You play baseball?" asked Pete.

"Sure," said Walter. "The Rockville League has a bunch of teams. We're on the Never Sink Nine."

"But without Billy we're only eight," said Melissa.

"I used to be on a team," Pete said softly. "Before we moved."

The Never Sink Nine teammates looked at each other. Everyone had the same thought in mind.

"Want to join our team?" Walter asked Pete. "We need another player."

"Sure!" said Pete. "Hear that, Homer?"

"Ba-a-a-a-a!"

"Homer says it's a *bat*-i-ful idea." Pete laughed at his own joke.

Melissa's eyes lit up. "Homer could be our mascot!"

"Yeah," said Christy. "He's home-run Homer!"

"I thought you wanted one of your toy horses to be our mascot," Mike said to Melissa.

"A real goat's better," Melissa said.

"Homer looks great in a uniform," said

Pete. He took off his baseball cap and stuck it on the goat's head.

Everyone laughed.

"Uh-oh," said Otis. "Here comes the Beanpole."

Becky and two of the Polar Blasts walked onto the playground. Recess had just begun.

"Look who's coming," said Melissa under her breath.

"Meet Homer," said Walter as Becky approached. "He's our team mascot."

"Beats your dumb old dog any day," said Otis.

Becky ignored him. "I heard you lost Billy Baskin. Are you ready to lose Saturday's game?"

"No way," said Walter. "We've got a new player. Don't worry. He'll be ready for Saturday's game."

Becky frowned. She shoved up one sleeve. The other two Polar Blasts did the same. "Do you have *tattoos*?" It sounded like a dare.

Walter couldn't believe it. All three

of them had polar bears tattooed on their arms!

"Wow!" said Otis. "Real tattoos!"

"I think they're ugly," said Christy.

Becky turned to leave. "By the way," she said. "Billy's a hard act to follow. Who's your new clean-up hitter?"

Walter couldn't wait to say it out loud. "Me," he said proudly.

Someone else said "Me" at the same time.

Walter looked at the person who thought he was going to take Billy's place instead of him.

It was Mike—his best friend!

CHAPTER THREE

Iron Mike

After school Walter ran straight to the bike rack outside Eleanor Roosevelt Elementary. He looked around for Mike. They were going to the batting cage together.

Walter spotted his friend near the jungle gym. Mike was talking to the new boy, Pete. They were petting Homer and laughing.

"Hey, Mike!" Walter yelled. But Mike didn't hear.

Walter checked his Babe Ruth watch.

The big bat pointed to ten. The little bat was on three.

Everyone in the Rockville League liked to practice hitting during baseball season. There were two batting cages next to Diamond Park. Walter knew they'd both be taken if he didn't get there fast.

I'll meet Mike there, he thought and pushed off.

Walter bicycled past Diamond Park and coasted around the back of Anderson's gas station. Two batting cages stood side by side.

Dave Johnson was hitting balls in the fast pitching cage. He was on Walter's brother Danny's team. The slow pitching cage was free.

"Hi, Dave," said Walter.

Dave nodded hello.

Walter dumped his bike and opened the chain-link fence to the slow cage. He dug around in his jeans pocket for change.

A metal box near the door read, 10 BALLS—50¢.

33

Walter shoved two quarters in a slot in the box. He picked up an aluminum bat leaning against the fence and closed the door. He held the bat over one shoulder and waited for the pitching machine to spit out the first ball.

Walter missed every ball. He could hear Dave smacking balls one after another. *It's because he's a fourth grader,* thought Walter.

When the machine clicked off, Walter put in two more quarters. He missed the first six balls. Then he made two hits.

Walter heard a voice.

"Nice going."

He turned around. Mike and Pete were standing outside the cage behind him, watching. While Walter's head was turned a ball sped past his shoulder. He swung at the last ball and missed.

"Where'd you go?" Walter asked Mike.

"Over to Pete's house," said Mike. "We had to drop off Homer." He said "we" as if he and Pete were already friends.

Dave Johnson came out of the fast batting cage. "Who's next?" he asked.

34

"Me," said Mike.

Dave handed Mike the bat.

"Don't you want to wait for my cage?" Walter asked. He and Mike had never batted in the fast cage.

"Coach said I should give the fast cage a try." Mike slipped his coins in and waited for the first ball. It shot out of the machine fast.

Mike swung and missed.

Walter shook his head. "You just wasted fifty cents."

Mike choked up on the bat and dug in. His eyes were glued to the pitching machine. When the next one shot out, Mike was ready.

He swung around hard and fast.

Tink!

A solid hit.

"Fantastic!" shouted Pete.

Walter dug the toe of his sneaker in the dirt. *Lucky hit,* he thought.

But Mike hit the next one, too. And the next and the next and the next until he hit seven out of the ten balls.

"That felt great," said Mike. "I like the

fast cage." He dug into his pocket for more change but he came up empty.

Walter knew he had money to lend his friend but he didn't say anything. Mike had never hit like that before. When had he gotten so good?

Mike stepped out of the cage.

"Iron Mike!" said Pete, clapping Mike on the back.

"What'd you call me?" asked Mike.

"Don't you know what an Iron Mike is?" asked Pete. "It's what they call the pitching machine."

"I knew that," lied Walter. He stepped out of the slow cage and let someone take his place. He didn't feel like hitting anymore.

"All the major leaguers have nicknames," said Pete. "I'm gonna call you Iron Mike!"

Mike burst into a smile. Walter watched his friend split his last piece of gum with the new boy.

"Wanna sleep over Friday night?" Pete

asked Mike. "We can wash Homer for the game."

"Yeah," said Mike. "I guess so. But I have to ask my mom first."

Walter felt tired. He wanted to go home. He got on his bike.

"Hey, where're you going?" Mike asked Walter.

"Home. I've got stuff to do."

"Later, alligator!" Mike yelled after him.

Walter didn't answer.

Walter took the shortcut home down Melrose Lane. He passed Melissa Nichols' house.

Melissa, her younger sister Jenny, and Katie Kessler were running through the sprinkler in their bathing suits. Melissa's toy horses stood in a circle all around the sprinkler.

"Hi, Walter!" Melissa shouted as he bicycled past.

"Babies," Walter said to himself. But he remembered how the cool water felt running down his arms and legs. Last summer he and Mike ran through the sprinkler almost every day.

Walter pulled into his driveway and walked across the lawn.

"Hey, watch it!"

His brother Danny was stretched out on the lawn. Walter had almost stepped on him.

"Why're you home?" asked Walter. Danny always went to Diamond Park after school.

"Too hot," said Danny. "Wanna hit a few?" He sat up and ground a baseball into his mitt.

Walter couldn't believe it. His big shot brother never played with him anymore— not since he joined the Flyers. Danny only played with fourth graders.

"Well, don't just stand there," said Danny. "Get my bat."

Walter trotted inside to get Danny's bat. Danny was a real slugger. Maybe he could help Walter be one, too.

Danny pitched three slow ones. Walter was late on the first two. He tagged the third.

"You're swinging wild," said Danny. "Stop trying for a grand slam and just get the bat on the ball."

Walter tried again but he wasn't much better.

"You're not trying," said Danny.

Walter lowered the bat. "I can't." He looked away. "I'll never be a hitter."

Walter waited for his brother to tease him. Instead, Danny walked across the lawn to him. "Wanna know how you can always hit the ball?"

Walter looked up at Danny and waited for the secret.

"One word," said Danny. "Bunt."

"Bunt?"

"You won't make a home run but it's a good shot at getting on first. And you'll always hit the ball."

You'll always hit the ball. The words sounded like magic.

"Will you teach me?" asked Walter. He tried not to show how much he cared.

"Sure," said Danny. "Even a turkey-brain brother oughta know how to bunt."

40

"Thanks," said Walter.

"First get me a soda," said Danny. "This coaching stuff is making me thirsty."

Walter didn't have to be asked twice. He ran into the house past his mother in the kitchen. He slid across the floor to the refrigerator and grabbed a soda.

"What's the hurry?" asked Mrs. Dodd.

"Danny wants a soda," said Walter. He couldn't waste time with small talk. Danny might change his mind.

"Can't he get his own soda?" she asked.

"He's teaching me to bunt!" said Walter as if that explained everything.

Danny spent the rest of the afternoon teaching him the basics of a good bunt.

"Start out like you're going to swing," said Danny. "At the last second hold the bat over the plate and just let the ball hit the bat."

By dinnertime Walter had it down pat.

"Time for dinner!" shouted Mr. Dodd.

Danny and Walter started inside together but Walter raced upstairs to his room. He needed to write in his Slugger Secrets notebook. He pulled it out of his back-pack and sat down on a heap of dirty clothes. His Never Sink Nine uniform was on top.

He added two secrets.

4. Don't trust best friends.
(especially Mike)
5. Be nice to your brother.
He can save your life.

Walter heard Danny shouting up the stairs. "Dinner, turkey-brain!"

"Coming!" shouted Walter.

He stuffed his dirty uniform under the bed so his mother couldn't wash out the good luck before the game. Then he raced down the stairs.

CHAPTER FOUR

Bats, Books, and the Babe

Pete Santos was sitting at Billy Baskin's old desk. He was so tall that he nearly blocked Walter's view of the blackboard.

"Blockhead," Walter whispered to himself. He leaned sideways to see the class homework assignment.

Walter looked across the aisle at Mike's bulging backpack. *It's probably full of sleepover stuff,* thought Walter. Today was Friday and Mike was sleeping over at Pete's. Walter felt left out.

43

Pete turned around and tossed a paper wad on Walter's desk.

Maybe he wants me to sleep over too, thought Walter. He quickly flattened out the note.

Walter's heart sank. He shook his head at Pete and looked out the classroom window.

Grandpa Walt's car pulled up in front of Eleanor Roosevelt Elementary. *At least I can count on* some *people,* he thought. Grandpa Walt had promised to buy him a new bat after school.

"Class dismissed," announced Mrs. Howard. "See you Monday."

Everyone headed for the door.

Walter watched Mike and Pete leave together.

Mike stopped at the door and looked back at Walter. "Want to go to Anderson's and hit some balls?"

"Can't," said Walter. "Grandpa Walt's buying me a new bat."

"Lucky," said Mike. "See you later, alligator."

"Bye, Walter," said Pete. "See you at the game."

Walter waited until they rode off on their bikes. Then he dashed out to Grandpa Walt's car.

Walter slid next to his grandfather on the car seat.

"Hi, little Walt."

"Hi, big Walt," said Walter.

Grandpa Walt turned the steering wheel and pulled out onto the street. "So, what's it going to be, aluminum or wood?"

"Wood," said Walter. He knew his grandfather was talking about baseball bats.

"Like the major leaguers, eh?" He winked at Walter.

Walter grinned. Grandpa Walt knew that was the only reason kids chose wood. Aluminum was lighter and hit farther.

"Know what brand?"

Walter rubbed the face of his Babe

45

Ruth watch. He wasn't sure. "What kind did the Babe use?"

"Probably a Louisville Slugger."

"That's what I want," said Walter.

"You got it." Grandpa Walt turned the car onto Main Street in downtown Rockville. "First stop, Swenson's Sporting Goods," announced Grandpa Walt like a real bus driver. He had driven a bus for thirty years before he retired.

Grandpa Walt pulled up in front of Swenson's and handed Walter a quarter. Walter leapt out of the car and put it into the parking meter. The arrow inside pointed to sixty minutes. *Good*, thought Walter. He followed his grandfather into the store.

Walter breathed deeply. The store smelled like brand new basketballs and leather mitts. Swenson's Sporting Goods was Walter's favorite store in the world.

"Hello there, Mr. Dodd," said a man behind the counter. It was Mr. Swenson. "Can I help you two athletes find something?"

"I know where they are," said Walter,

leading the way. He knew where everything was. He headed straight for the back wall.

There they were. Dozens and dozens of brand-new baseball bats lined up in a row. Walter touched the handle of a Louisville Slugger. A chill went up his back.

Grandpa Walt joined him. "Which one's going to be the lucky winner?"

Walter grabbed the largest bat he could find. It had *4* stamped on the end of the handle. Walter knew that meant thirty-four inches.

"Whoa!" said Grandpa Walt. He lifted the heavy bat. "A bigger bat doesn't mean a bigger hit. Pick the right size for *you*."

"I'm medium," said Walter.

Grandpa Walt looked through the bats. He pulled out a twenty-seven incher. "How does this feel?"

Walter lifted it over one shoulder. It felt much lighter.

"The shorter the bat the faster you swing," said Grandpa Walt. "Danny's old bat was too big."

Walter took a practice swing. It felt

47

great. Light and fast. He felt in control for the first time.

"This is it," said Walter.

"Knock on wood." Grandpa Walt gave the wooden bat a rap with his knuckle.

Walter gave it a rap for good luck, too. He'd need all the luck he could get for tomorrow's game.

Grandpa Walt took Walter to Chung's Restaurant to celebrate.

Walter set his new bat on its own chair. Then he ordered his favorite dish, chicken with snow peas.

Christy Chung and her family were having dinner at a table nearby. The Chungs owned the restaurant. Christy stopped at Walter's table.

"Neat new bat," said Christy. "Think it'll help your hitting?"

Walter's ears started to burn. He took a bite of chicken and tried to ignore her.

"Finish your book report yet?" she asked, leaning over the table.

Walter looked down at his plate. "What do you care?"

"What's it about?" she asked.

"Something better than ballet," he said.

"Nothing's better than ballet," Christy said, as she did a graceful turn and walked on tiptoes back to her table.

"What *is* your book report about?" asked Grandpa Walt.

"Nothing special."

"Well I know something special," said Grandpa Walt. "I asked your mother if you could sleep over tonight."

Walter's eyes lit up. "What did she say?"

Grandpa Walt nodded his head *yes*.

Walter jumped up and down in his chair. "Yeah!" He loved spending the night at Grandpa Walt's apartment. It was right above Chung's Restaurant.

That night Walter put on one of his grandfather's pajama tops and climbed into the big bed. Grandpa Walt had on his reading glasses and was reading a book. Walter watched him for a few minutes. Then he let out a loud sigh.

Grandpa Walt looked down at Walter.

"You need something to read." He got out of bed and disappeared into the living room. In a few minutes he returned with an old book. A photograph slipped out from between the pages onto the bed.

Walter picked it up. It was a photo of a fat man in a baseball uniform. "Who's he?"

"Don't you recognize your hero?" asked Grandpa Walt. "That's Babe Ruth."

Walter couldn't believe it. He didn't look anything like the picture on his Babe Ruth watch.

Grandpa Walt handed the book to Walter. "It's good," he said. "Lots of pictures."

Walter read the title. *Babe Ruth: An American Hero.*

Walter couldn't wait to read about his hero. Some of the words were hard but that didn't stop him. He either asked his grandfather or figured out what they meant by the rest of the sentence.

He found out that Babe Ruth's real name was George Herman Ruth, Jr. and he grew up in an orphanage. Some of his nicknames were the Sultan of Swat, the Home

Run King, and the Bambino. He was left-handed.

"Guess what?" said Walter. "Babe wasn't a good reader either. And he didn't always hit the ball."

"It takes time to develop a batting style," said Grandpa Walt.

Finally Grandpa Walt took off his reading glasses. "You can finish that book at home."

Walter closed the book carefully and put it beside his new bat. Christy was wrong. He wouldn't flunk. He'd do his book report on Babe Ruth.

Grandpa Walt turned out the light. "We need lots of sleep before our big game tomorrow," he said.

"We'll melt those Polar Blasts," said Walter, snuggling under the covers.

"Night, little Walt," said his grandfather.

"Night, big Walt," said Walter.

CHAPTER FIVE

The Polar Blasts Game

Walter sat in the Never Sink Nine dugout fanning himself with his baseball cap. He wished he'd remembered to bring his water pistol. He was thirsty and the game hadn't even started yet.

Grandpa Walt carried a cooler into the dugout. "We'll need these today," he said, flipping open the lid. Inside were enough ice-cold sodas for everyone to have two sodas apiece.

Walter decided on grape and cherry.

Pete grabbed a piece of ice from the

cooler and dropped it into Homer's water bucket. The goat was wearing a team cap and T-shirt.

Grandpa Walt looked at the goat. "We've got the best-dressed mascot in the league."

Homer lifted his head. "Ba-a-a-a!"

Tony held up a drawing of Beanpole Becky. "Show them what we're gonna do to the Polar Blasts, Homer."

The goat sniffed the picture and took a big bite.

Everyone laughed as Homer happily tore up the competition.

Mike lifted Walter's new Louisville Slugger out of his backpack. "What a beauty," said Mike. "Bet you can't wait to use it."

"What do you care?" said Walter.

Mike put down the bat and stared at Walter.

The Polar Blasts' coach signaled to Grandpa Walt. The game was about to begin.

"Okay, team," said Grandpa Walt. "The

Polar Blasts are going to bat first. Let's hit the field."

Walter grabbed his mitt. He'd have to wait a little longer to use his new bat. He pulled on his baseball cap and jogged onto the field. He took his usual place at second base.

Mike was still staring at him from shortstop. Pete was on first.

The Polar Blasts got one run in the first inning. Then it was the Never Sink Nine's turn at bat.

Each one of the first three players in the batting lineup got a hit. The bases were loaded when Grandpa Walt called Mike up to bat.

"Congratulations," said Pete, shaking Mike's hand. "You're the clean-up batter."

Mike chose a gray aluminum bat and stepped up to the plate. He took a few practice swings.

"Clean 'em up!" yelled Otis. He was eating a bar of chocolate.

"Don't you ever close your mouth when

you eat?" snapped Walter. He had hoped *he'd* be clean-up batter.

Otis opened his mouth wider.

Walter ignored him. His eyes were glued on Mike.

Mike tapped the outside corner of the plate with his bat.

Becky was pitching for the Polar Blasts. She pumped up one leg and fired a high fastball over home plate.

Mike chopped down on the ball and missed. "Strike one!" The umpire held up a finger.

"Keep a level swing!" shouted Grandpa Walt.

The second pitch was just as fast. Mike let it slip past without moving a muscle. "Strike two!"

The bat slipped from Mike's hands. He picked it up quickly. Walter could see he was nervous.

"It's okay!" shouted Grandpa Walt. "You're just warming up!"

Last week Walter would have cheered his friend on. Now he was secretly hoping

Mike wouldn't do so well. Walter rolled his new bat between his hands. He'd show everyone who the real hitter on this team was. He looked at the batting glove and wristbands he'd borrowed from Danny. He felt like a real pro.

Mike flexed his knees. He shifted back and forth as he got ready to hit.

Becky wound up and pitched a low ball. Mike bent down to meet it. He whipped the bat around with all his might.

Ting!

It was a line drive to the outfield.

Pete jumped up on the bench. "Go, Mike!" he shouted.

Walter watched Mike round first and head for second base. The second baseman raised his mitt for the catch. Mike slid into second as the ball sank into his mitt.

"Safe!" shouted the umpire.

Melissa ran across home plate with Christy running right behind. Mike had forced in two runs!

"Lucky hit," said Becky from the pitcher's mound.

"What's wrong?" shouted Mike from second. "Can't take the heat?"

Becky pretended not to hear. She shoved up a sleeve so her polar bear tattoo showed. "Next batter!" she said, slapping the ball in her mitt.

Grandpa Walt turned to Tony. "Who's up next?"

Tony Pappas looked up from his drawing and pointed to Walter. "Dodd," he said and went back to drawing.

Walter wished he could disappear. How could he beat Mike's double? He'd have to hit a *triple*.

Walter pulled up his lucky socks. "Triple, triple, triple, triple, triple," he whispered to himself. He grabbed his Louisville Slugger and took a deep breath.

"Go get 'em, Walter!"

Mike was cheering him on from second base.

I'm going to be the home-run hero on this team, Walter thought. He gave his Babe Ruth watch a pat for luck. He swung his

bat over one shoulder and waited for the pitch.

Becky took a slow windup and fired the first ball.

Walter whipped the bat around so fast he lost his balance. He fell to his knees.

"Strike one!"

Walter dusted off his pants and dug in at home plate. He wasn't going to go down again no matter what. He took a wide swing at the next ball.

Swooooosh!

Grandpa Walt leaned forward. "You don't have to knock the stuffing out of a ball to get a hit," he said. "Relax."

Walter squeezed his bat so tight his knuckles turned white. He froze as the last ball whistled past into the catcher's mitt.

"Strike three!"

Walter dragged his bat back into the dugout.

"Good try," said Melissa.

Walter sank onto the bench and gave his bat a kick. "I whiffed."

"You weirdo," said Christy. "In case you

haven't noticed we've all struck out too. What makes you so special?"

Walter looked at his teammates all lined up on the bench waiting to hit. Christy was right. Every one of them had struck out at one time or another.

CHAPTER 6

Slugger Secrets

It was a close game. The score had been even in almost every inning. Now it was the bottom of the sixth. Walter glanced up at the scoreboard. The score was 6–6.

A big drop of water splashed on Walter's face. He looked up at the sky. Big dark storm clouds were moving over Diamond Park.

"Hurry up!" shouted Grandpa Walt. "Let's break this tie before we're rained out!"

Walter ran toward the dugout. Maybe it would rain before his turn up at bat!

Walter took a seat far away from Mike on the dugout bench. "Rain, rain, rain, rain, rain," he whispered five times for luck. He hoped the drizzle would turn into a downpour.

Suddenly Mike moved over next to Walter. "What's wrong?" he said.

Walter looked away. "What are you talking about?" he mumbled.

"You've been acting weird," Mike said. "Don't you want to be friends anymore?"

Walter couldn't believe his ears. That's how *he* had felt all week! He stared at Mike. "I thought *you* didn't want to be friends. You're with Pete all the time."

Mike shook his head. "Pete's funny and I like him. But you're my best friend." He looked down. "I thought maybe you didn't like it because I'm hitting better."

"No," Walter lied. But he couldn't look Mike in the eye.

Grandpa Walt walked over to them. "You're up next, Mike. We've got two out. Try to get on base." He turned to Walter. "It's your job to drive Mike in."

"We can do it," said Mike. "Right, Dodd?"

"Right, Lasky." Walter forced a smile.

Mike jumped up and ran to the batter's box. Walter watched him fumbling to put on his batting helmet. *Mike needs to know his team's behind him,* he thought. Walter clapped his hands and shouted as loud as he could, "Slug it, Mike!"

Mike looked back at Walter and smiled.

Suddenly Walter didn't care if they won or not. He had his best friend back.

Becky fired the first pitch.

Mike whipped the bat around in a level swing.

Ting! It was a solid hit to left field.

Mike made it to third base before the outfielder made the play. The Never Sink Nine were cheering their heads off. And Walter was screaming the loudest.

Grandpa Walt walked over to Walter.

"It's up to you, champ. Two out and the score's tied."

"If you knock Mike in we'll win!" said Christy. She stood on her toes and twirled like a ballerina.

Walter grabbed his bat and headed for home plate.

One big raindrop splashed onto Walter's face. He squinted to see Mike on third. He had to drive him in for the team. But how?

He took a deep breath. A cool breeze swept over the field. The heat wave had broken. A chill went up his spine.

"Let's get this over with," said Becky from the pitcher's mound. Her hair hung down in long wet strings.

Walter gripped his bat and waited for the first pitch. He swung hard at the ball.

Swooooosh!

"Strike!"

"You don't have to kill it!" shouted Melissa from the dugout. "Just get a hit!"

Suddenly Walter remembered the magic word his brother Danny had taught him. You'll always hit the ball, he'd said.

65

Bunt.

Walter put down his bat and gave his lucky socks a hard yank. *Bunt, bunt, bunt, bunt, bunt,* he thought. He knew he had to get the bunt past Becky. That would give Mike time to run home.

The next ball was slow and easy.

Walter waited until the last second and squared off his bat. He bunted the ball down the third-base line. It rolled out of Becky's reach.

Mike ran for home plate as fast as he could.

The third baseman scooped up the ball.

"Throw it home!" Becky yelled to the third baseman.

"Slide!" Grandpa Walt yelled to Mike.

Mike dove for the plate. The ball sailed toward the catcher's mitt. Mike's hand touched home plate.

"Safe!" the umpire shouted. "Game's over! Let's get out of this rain!" He ran for cover as thunderclouds broke open and rain came pouring down.

The Never Sink Nine burst out of the dugout onto the field. All the players threw their baseball caps and mitts into the air.

Otis opened the cooler and started drinking sodas. He shook up two cans of orange soda and sprayed them over Mike and Walter's heads. No one cared that they were getting soaked.

Becky and some of the Polar Blasts raced past with their team mascot. Blue ink was running down their arms.

"Hey, look!" shouted Tony. "Their big-shot tattoos were phony!"

"And look at their polar bear," said Melissa.

The polar bear's fluffy white fur was plastered to his skin from the rain. He looked like a skinny wet dishrag.

Homer ran after the dog. "Ba-a-a-a!"

"Homer knows the Polar Blasts are a lot of hot air," said Pete.

"Yeah," said Walter.

Everyone laughed as Homer chased the Polar Blasts off the field.

Then Grandpa Walt took a team photo

on home plate. He took a picture at just about every game. Walter and Mike put their arms around each other's shoulders. Everyone looked muddy, wet, and happy. Even Homer looked like he was smiling.

"All aboard for the Pizza Palace!" said Grandpa Walt, pulling up in his station wagon. Everyone piled in.

It was Otis's turn to choose pizza. He wanted the super deluxe with everything. But the rules were you could only choose three toppings. He picked cheese and sausage with black olives.

When everyone finished Christy started a team cheer.

"Three, Five, Seven, Nine
Who's the winner rain or shine?
Never Sink! Never Sink! Never Sink Nine!"

Everyone joined in the cheer.

Then Grandpa Walt treated the team to ice cream. Homer had to wait outside, because goats weren't allowed inside. Pete tied his rope to a parking meter and the team sat at a table in the window to keep an eye on him. Walter and Mike shared a banana split. They split everything down the middle, including the cherry.

Tony gave Pete his new team baseball card. He had already made baseball cards for everyone else in the Never Sink Nine. They looked just like the major-league cards.

Tony gave Walter a picture of him making the winning bunt. Mike got a picture of himself sliding into home.

Mike autographed his picture and shoved it toward Walter. "Let's trade," he said.

"Great." Walter signed his name on his picture and gave it to Mike. "We'll always be major-league friends," he said.

After a while Grandpa Walt got up and paid the check. "The Never Sink Nine Express is leaving in one minute!" he called. Everyone followed him into the parking lot.

Mike and Walter were the last to be dropped off. "Next stop, the Lasky house," announced Grandpa Walt, bus-driver-style.

Mike jumped out of the car into the rain. "See you later, alligator." He made a dash for his house.

"In a while, crocodile!" Walter shouted after his friend. He leaned back against Grandpa Walt. He was nearly asleep when they pulled up in front of his house.

"Last stop, the Dodd house," Grandpa Walt announced.

Walter opened his eyes and looked down. The picture of Mike sliding home rested in his lap. Mike had stuck a wad of gum near his name in one corner.

Grandpa Walt looked at Mike's autograph. "Looks like you're Mike's biggest fan."

Walter smiled. "He's mine, too."

"That's the way best friends ought to be," said Grandpa Walt. He gave Walter a good-bye hug. "Practice your pitching, champ. You'll share the mound with Melissa next week. We're playing the Bug Busters."

Walter made a dash for the front door. He raced up to his room and taped Mike's picture over his bed.

Walter pulled the Slugger Secrets notebook out of his backpack and sat down on his bed. He had some important changes to make. He crossed off the first word of number four, so that it now read, Trust best friends. (Especially Mike).

Then he added number six: 6. You don't have to be a home-run hitter to win the game. Bunt.

Walter grabbed his Babe Ruth book from under his pillow. He was sure somewhere it said the Babe was a pitcher before he was a hitter. He needed to read all about it before next week's game.

I'll have the best book report in class, thought Walter.

He opened his book and started to read.

Tony's Tips on How to Make Your Own Baseball Cards

1. Get a teammate to take a 3″ x 5″ snapshot of you wearing your team uniform. Pretend to be pitching, catching, or batting.

2. Trim off the edges of your snapshot and paste it on a piece of white paper. Draw a quarter-inch border all around the snapshot. Color it in with your team colors.

3. Print your name, field position, and team number on the bottom border, and the year on the upper right-hand part of the border.

4. Now copy as many as you want. You may need help reducing the copied picture to baseball card size. (You can either make a color copy or use colored pencils to add color yourself.)

5. Cut out the completed copy and paste on white posterboard or cardboard. Trim to fit.

6. Keep your team statistics on the back of your card.

ABOUT THE AUTHOR

GIBBS DAVIS was born in Milwaukee, Wisconsin, graduated from the University of California at Berkeley, and lives in New York City. She has published *Swann Song*, a young adult novel, with Avon Books, *Walter's Lucky Socks* and *Major-League Melissa* are the first two books in The Never Sink Nine series for First Skylark.

ABOUT THE ILLUSTRATOR

GEORGE ULRICH was born in Morristown, New Jersey, and received his Bachelor of Fine Arts from Syracuse University. He has illustrated several Bantam Skylark books, including *Make Four Million Dollars by Next Thursday!* by Stephen Manes and *The Amazing Adventure of Me, Myself, and I* by Jovial Bob Stine. He lives in Marblehead, Massachusetts, with his wife and two sons.